THE FEELINGS BOOK

TODD PARR

Megan Tingley Books

LITTLE, BROWN AND COMPANY

NEW YORK BOSTON

Little, Brown and Company

Hachette Book Group
1290 Avenue of the Americas, New York, NY 10104
Visit our website at www.lb-kids.com

Little, Brown and Company is a division of Hachette Book Group, Inc.
The Little, Brown name and logo are trademarks of Hachette Book Group, Inc.

First Paperback Edition: April 2009
Originally published in hardcover in September 2000 by Little, Brown and Company.

Library of Congress Cataloging-in-Publication Data

Parr, Todd.
  The feelings book / Todd Parr.—1st ed.
    p. cm.
  Summary: Children express different moods, including "I feel very mad,"
"I feel like reading books all day," and "I feel like wearing funny underwear."
  [1. Emotions—Fiction.]   I. Title.
  PZ7.P2447Fe   2000
  [E]—dc21   99-42775
  ISBN-13: 978-0-316-04346-5

21

IM

Printed in China

This book is dedicated to
Dad, Tammy, Sandy, Sara, Dawn, Bryan, Bill,
Candy, Jerry, Liz and Gerry, John and Linda
Alioto, Maggie W., Jeff and Steve, Jim and
Jean, Bully, Mow, Isabel and Benny, Michael,
Artt, Megan, Cindy Sue, Kerri, Stacey, Linda,
and everyone at Little, Brown.

Love,
Todd

Sometimes I feel silly.

Sometimes I feel cranky.

Sometimes I feel scared.

Sometimes I feel like standing on my head.

Sometimes I feel like reading a book under the covers.

Sometimes I feel like celebrating my birthday,

even though
it's not today.

Sometimes I feel brave.

Sometimes I feel like looking out the window all day.

Sometimes I feel

like dancing.

Sometimes I feel
like making mudpies.

Sometimes I feel like
I have a tummy ache.

Sometimes I feel like holding hands with a friend.

Sometimes I feel lonely.

Sometimes I feel like yelling really loud.

Sometimes I feel like staying in the bathtub all day.

Sometimes I feel like trying something new.

Sometimes I feel like dressing up.

Sometimes I feel

like doing nothing.

Sometimes I feel like camping with my dog.

Sometimes I feel
like crying.

Sometimes I feel like eating pizza for breakfast.

Sometimes I feel like kissing a sea lion.

Sometimes I feel
like a king.

No matter how you feel, don't keep your feelings to yourself. Share them with someone you love.

Love,
Todd